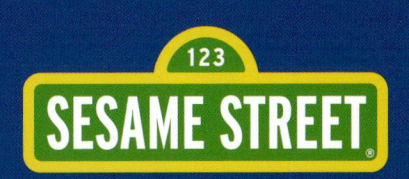

WELCOME TO BRAZIL WITH SESAME STREET

CHRISTY PETERSON

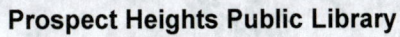

Lerner Publications ◆ Minneapolis

In this series, *Sesame Street* characters help readers learn about other countries' people, cultures, landscapes, and more. These books connect friends around the world while giving readers new tools to become smarter, kinder friends. Pack your bags and take a fun-filled look at your world with your funny, furry friends from *Sesame Street.*

—Sincerely, the Editors at Sesame Street

TABLE OF CONTENTS

Welcome to Brazil! 4

Where in the World Is Brazil? 6

Fast Facts 21
Glossary 22
Learn More 23
Index 24

WELCOME TO BRAZIL!

Ola, my name is Bel. I live in Brazil.

Brazil is the largest country in South America. Most people there speak Portuguese.

WHERE IN THE WORLD IS BRAZIL?

NORTH AMERICA

ATLANTIC OCEAN

PACIFIC OCEAN

SOUTH AMERICA

Brazil

VENEZUELA
COLOMBIA
GUYANA
SURINAME
FRENCH GUIANA
ATLANTIC OCEAN
PERU
BRAZIL
Brasilia
BOLIVIA
PACIFIC OCEAN
PARAGUAY
ARGENTINA
URUGUAY

Miles
0 200 400
0 200 400
Kilometers

Brazil and Surrounding Area

ARCTIC OCEAN

ASIA

EUROPE

AFRICA

PACIFIC OCEAN

INDIAN OCEAN

AUSTRALIA

SOUTHERN OCEAN

7

The Amazon rain forest covers much of Brazil. Brazil also has beautiful mountains and beaches.

The Pantanal is the world's largest tropical wetland. Jaguars and giant anteaters live there!

Many people live in cities. Families might live in houses or apartment buildings.

Some people live on farms.

Some families live in the rain forest!

Dancing is part of Carnival. One dance is called the *samba*.

Carnival is a popular holiday. Some people dress up and march in parades. Others dance in their neighborhoods.

12

Elmo likes *frevo*! It's another kind of dance.

13

Children's Day is another important holiday. Kids and their families have fun and enjoy the day together.

Children's Day is called *Dia das Criancas* in Brazil!

15

People like to spend time with their relatives. Grandparents often take care of their grandchildren.

Look at those happy families. I'll stay in my trash can!

Families often eat rice and beans with meat. *Feijoada* is one popular dish. People also enjoy fruits.

Me want to try passion fruit. Yum!

19

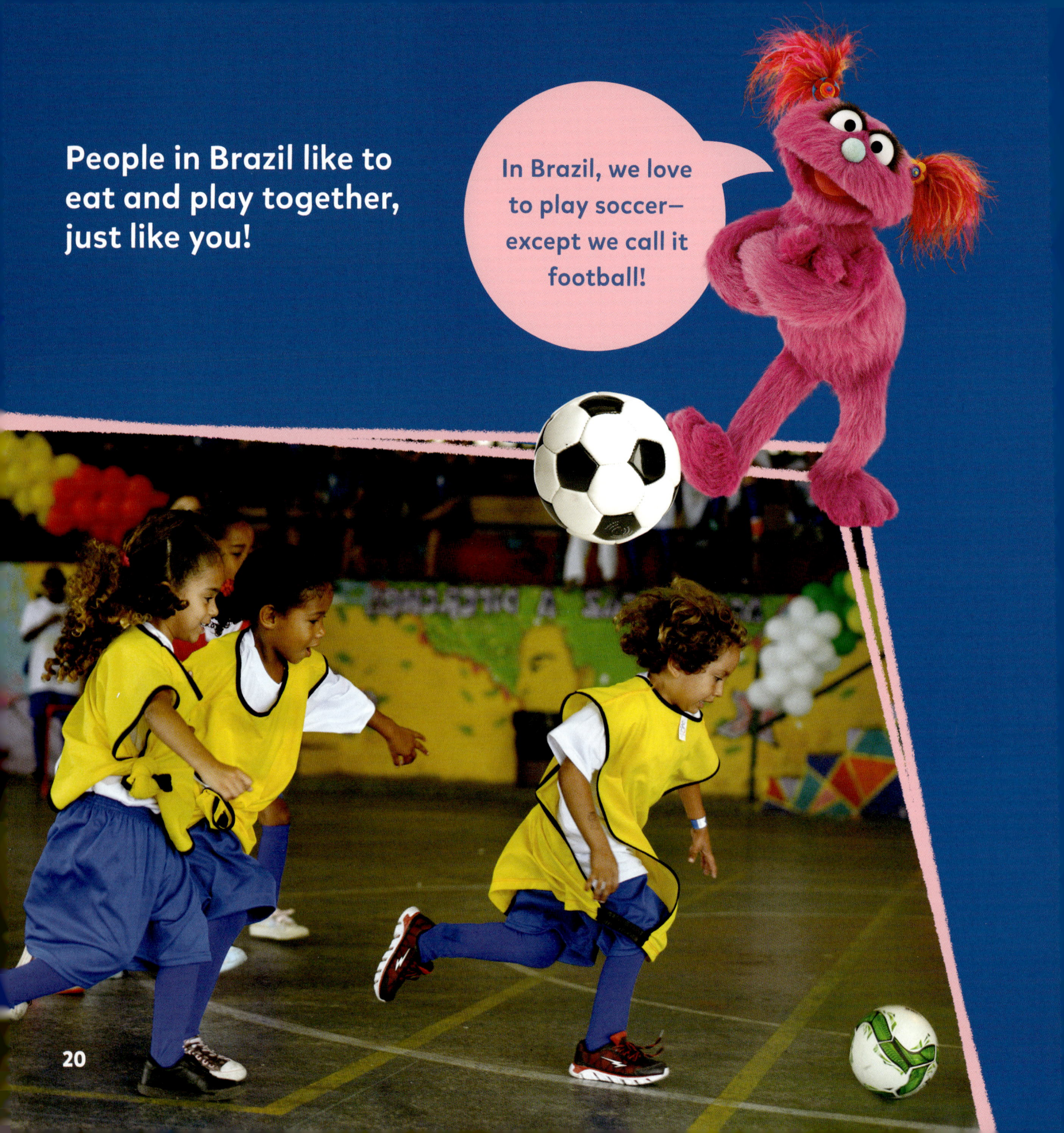

People in Brazil like to eat and play together, just like you!

In Brazil, we love to play soccer—except we call it football!

Flag of Brazil

FAST FACTS

Continent: South America

Capital city: Brasilia

Population: 208.8 million

Language: Portuguese

21

GLOSSARY

feijoada: a dish made of black beans, rice, meat, cassava flour, kale, and slices of orange

Pantanal: a large area in South America that floods in summer and is swampy most of the year

rain forest: a forest that gets a lot of rain all year

relative: someone who is related, such as a grandparent, aunt, uncle, or cousin

tropical: related to the tropics, or warm, humid places near the equator